Thawing Frozen Frogs

Poems by Brian Patten

Illustrated by David Mostyn

PUFFIN BOOKS

PUFFIN BOOKS

Published by the Penguin Group
Penguin Books Ltd, 27 Wrights Lane, London W8 5TZ, England
Penguin Books USA Inc., 375 Hudson Street, New York, New York 10014, USA
Penguin Books Australia Ltd, Ringwood, Victoria, Australia
Penguin Books Canada Ltd, 10 Alcorn Avenue, Toronto, Ontario, Canada M4V 3B2
Penguin Books (NZ) Ltd, 182–190 Wairau Road, Auckland 10, New Zealand

Penguin Books Ltd, Registered Offices: Harmondsworth, Middlesex, England

First published by Viking 1990
Published in Puffin Books 1992
1 3 5 7 9 10 8 6 4 2

Text copyright © Brian Patten, 1990
Illustrations copyright © David Mostyn, 1990
All rights reserved

Printed in England by Clays Ltd, St Ives plc
Filmset in Photina

PUFFIN BOOKS

THAWING FROZEN FROGS

Witty, imaginative and often outrageous, only Brian Patten could have created this rich and varied sequel to his infamous *Gargling with Jelly*. Enter his marvellous, manic and mad world of rebellious children and hard-done-by adults, where comic and serious poems collide in another exhilarating collection.

Brian Patten was born in Liverpool in 1946. His poetry for adults has been published in many languages and his collections include *Love Poems*, *Storm Damage* and *Grinning Jack*. As well as his poetry collections, his work for children includes children's plays and the award-winning novel, *Mr Moon's Last Case*.

Also by Brian Patten

GARGLING WITH JELLY
JIMMY TAG-ALONG
MR MOON'S LAST CASE
THE PUFFIN BOOK OF TWENTIETH CENTURY
CHILDREN'S VERSE (ed.)

Contents

Growing Groany

Grown-ups are groan-ups, there's no doubt about it,
You can tell by the way they groan on about it.

The Giant's Family Dinner

For dinner I had a little boy,
He tasted rather funny.
I spat him out right away
Because his nose was runny.

Next I tried a little girl
(They are supposed to taste nicer)
But I broke my tooth because
I'd forgotten to de-ice her.

By now I was quite peckish
So I tried a leg-of-dad,
As it was past the sell-by date
It tasted rather bad.

I nibbled on a mother,
But wanting something new
I boiled a bit of granny
And tried some uncle-stew.

I did not eat the baby –
That was out the question
(And anyway they wriggle
And cause indigestion).

Usually I eat alone
In a huge and draughty hall.
Having a family for dinner
Is not to my taste at all.

Schoolitis

You haven't got a cough,
You haven't got mumps,
You haven't got a chill
Or any funny lumps.
You haven't got a tummy-ache,
You haven't got a fever,
You haven't got a runny nose
Or chicken-pox either.
You don't look a ruin,
You don't look a wreck,
You haven't got toothache
Or a pain in the neck.
You're fit as a fiddle,
You're sound as a bell,
In fact I've never ever
Seen you looking so well!
You don't fool me,
I'm no fool.
Now up out of bed
AND OFF TO SCHOOL!

The Invisible Man's Invisible Dog

My invisible dog is not much fun.
I don't know if he's sad or glum.
I don't know if, when I pat his head,
I'm really patting his bum instead.

Hairy Fairy

I saw a hairy fairy
Doing press-ups in the gym.
He sweated quite profusely
So I went and said to him,
'Though you are sensational
I find it irrational
To see a hairy fairy
Panting so profusely
With his track-suit hanging loosely
Doing press-ups in the gym.'

The Teachercreature

We held a seance in the kitchen,
Me, Jenny and Jo.
We covered the table with an old stained cloth
And turned the lights down low.
We summoned up a poltergeist,
A witch and a wizard too,
We summoned up a goblin
And an imp or two.
We summoned up a vampire,
A werewolf and a ghoul,
We summoned up a banshee
With a fearful howl.
Our hair turned grey, our knees gave way,
We trembled and felt sweaty,
And then we went and summoned up
A zombie and a yeti.
We summoned up a spectre,
A phantom and a spook,
We summoned up things so bad
We were scared to look.
Then last of all we summoned up
The world's most frightful creature.
We dashed out of the room because
It was our old schoolteacher.

I'm Going to Be an Environmentalist When I Learn What to Do With the Greenfly

There's a gorilla in the wardrobe,
It must be from the zoo.
It's that or a fur-coat
Mum's hidden from view.
She's become a green
  Environmental Mum,
    She'll not be seen dead
      With that gorilla on!

Down in the garden,
Hidden in the shed,
Dad's gone and stashed away
A tatty fox's head.
He's become a green
Preservational Dad.
All those baby foxes
Must be feeling glad!

I hear that spraying greenfly
Has become an issue,
So I've been round the garden
Wrapping them in tissue.
I'd be as green as anyone
If I knew what to do.
Should I squeeze the greenfly gently,
Or flush them down the loo?

The Owl's Trick

From its hollow and ancient tree
An owl looked down and said to me:

'About my feet are swarms of mice –
I can easily leave them there,
For from their feet I've ripped their toes
And now they'll not go anywhere.

I eat them slowly at my ease,
I pick and choose them as I please.
The fattest one I let digest
Before indulging in the rest.

I bring them corn into my croft,
It keeps them both alive and soft.
Before this trick occurred to me
They were nimble and scurried free.

I've neatly torn the paws from each
Panicking creature in my reach;
No doubt you think I'm cruel, but then
Who invented the battery-hen?'

The Mouse's Invitation Cards

'Come at seven,' 'Come at nine,'
'Come whenever you want.'
On the shelf the printed cards
Seem kind in their intent.

But the mouse will always stay at home,
He will never venture out,
No matter how the cards insist
Friends are all about.

One's from a cat, one's from an owl,
And both are intent
To draw him from his nest and then
Have him where they want.

The Pet Wig

Our teacher has a pet wig,
Nobody knows its name,
It clings to his baldy head
And looks extremely tame.

It's very calm and patient.
When dogs are on the prowl
It pretends it cannot hear the way
They clear their throats and growl.

It comes from a far-off land
(Or so we like to think),
A strange endangered species
That's just about extinct.

After school he takes it off
And offers it some milk.
He strokes it extra gently
(Its fur is smooth as silk).

And in his lonely room at night
When he decides to retire,
He lays it down quite carefully
On a blanket near the fire.

After a long day clinging,
It rests content and purring.

The Race to Get to Sleep

They're on their marks, they're set,
They're off!

Matthew's kicking off his shoes!
Penny's struggling out of her jumper!
He's ripping off his trousers!
She's got one sock off! Now the other's off!
But Matthew's still winning! No, he's not!
It's Penny! Penny's in the lead!
She's down to her knickers!
She's racing out of the room!
She's racing upstairs!
Matthew's right behind her!
There's a fight on the landing!
There's a scramble at the bathroom door!
It's Penny! It's Matthew! It's . . .
Splash! They're both in the bath!
But there's a hitch!
Matthew's got soap in his eye!
Penny's got soap up her nose!
They're stalling! But no, they're both fine!
They're both out the bath! They're neck and neck!
It's Matthew! It's Penny! It's Matthew!
Now it's Penny again! She's ahead!
She's first on with her pyjamas!
Now Matthew's catching up! There's nothing in it!
They're climbing into their beds!
Matthew's in the lead with one eye closed!
Now it's Penny again! She's got both closed!

So's Matthew! He's catching up!
It's impossible to tell who's winning!
They're both absolutely quiet!
There's not a murmur from either of them.
It's Matthew! It's Penny! It's . . .
It's a draw! A draw!
But no! Wait a moment! It's not a draw!
Matthew's opened an eye!
He's asking if Penny's asleep yet!
He's disqualified!
So's Penny! She's doing the same!
She's asking if Matthew's asleep yet!
It's impossible! It's daft!
It's the hardest race in the world!

Ten Angels Alone on Trapezes

I saw ten angels alone on trapezes,
Nine monkeys dancing in fire,
I saw eight snowflakes falling in lakes
And seven fish caught on a wire.

I saw six pirates with sacks full of treasure,
Five tigers sharing a crust,
Four budgerigars playing guitars
And three blackthorns covered in dust.

I saw two shadows without any owners,
One faded and then was gone,
Its friend searched for it in the darkness,
And then, of course, there were none.

The Experiment

I did an experiment to prove groan-ups
Don't pay much attention to kids.

To the first groan-up I said,
'That rabbit over there's just eaten a mouse!'

He said,
'Well, I never.'

To the second groan-up I said,
'The cat's just cooked itself some dinner!'

She said,
'Well, I never.'

Then I dashed out of the house yelling,
'There's an elephant just about to fall on the roof!'

And they both said,
'Well, I nev–'
SPLAT!!!!

Gran Says

Gran says her friend Pat
Has a bee in her bonnet.
So I smeared honey on it.

Gran says her friend Mary
Is thick as two short planks.
She isn't. She's fat as two ten-ton tanks.

Gran says her friend Alice
Is always carrying a Grudge.
I looked in her shopping-bag –
There wasn't one measly little Grudge in it.
I said, 'Don't budge, you've lost your Grudge!
Make sure Mary doesn't sit on it!
Catch it with Pat's sticky bonnet!'
Everyone thought I was mad.

Gran says her friend Clare
Leads a dog's life.
If so, why did she spit out
The winnowmeat sandwich I made her?

Gran says her friend Stan
Has a chip on his shoulder.
It's not true. When I saw him, I said,

'Has someone eaten your chip, Stan?'
He sort of frowned at Gran.

Gran says her friend Arthur
Thinks he's Lord Muck.
So that's what I called him
(And I bowed).
I don't know why Gran and him rowed.

Gran says her friend Joan
Needs her head examined.
Last time I saw her, I said,
'Sorry to hear about the nits.'

Now, whenever I visit Gran,
If her friends are there
She has fits.

One Reason I Love Grandad

'You're worthless!' Gran complains,
Glaring at the fruitbowl in disgust.

'What do you mean, I'm worthlesh?'
Says Grandad, his false teeth still embedded
In the apple he's just put back,
Absent-mindedly, into the fruitbowl.

'Worthlesh – me!
I'm worth my weight in bush-pashes.'

Acid Snow Drops

How deep the snow,
How white it falls,
How cold and sharp the air,
How perfectly each little flake
Pollutes the atmosphere.

It's Poisoning Down

Granny keeps telling stories
Of how she used to go
Walking in the pouring rain
And playing in the snow.
She talks of things called flowers,
She says they had nice smells,
(Sometimes she sounds convincing,
The crazy fibs she tells!).
She says that lakes and rivers
Were once all clean and pure,
But I don't believe a word,
I've heard it all before.
Poor Gran can be quite dotty –
You want to see Mum frown
When Gran tries to get outside
Even though it's poisoning down.

We've had to fit 'Granny Locks'
To keep poor Granny in.
She really doesn't understand
How rain eats away the skin.

The Milk-shake Cafe

I went into the milk-shake cafe
And saw the milk-shake cows,
They stood behind the counter
In different-flavoured rows.

The banana-flavoured milk-shake cow
Ate bananas by the bunch,
The raspberry-flavoured milk-shake cow
Had raspberries for lunch.

The lemon-flavoured milk-shake cow
Sulked and spat out pips,
The orange-flavoured milk-shake cow
Had orange-coloured lips.

To get the milk-shakes frothy
There was a strange machine
That shook the mooing cows
And turned their milk to cream.

There were so many different flavours
We were spoilt for choice,
Until one day the owner said
In a trembly sort of voice,

'Quick! Clear out the cafe
I've just been told today,
The place is being raided
By the RSPCA.'

Mary Had a Bit of Lamb

Mary had a little lamb,
Its fleece was white as snow,
And everywhere that Mary went
The lamb was sure to go.

She went into the butcher's,
Came out with some lamb chops.
I would never follow Mary
Into any kind of shops!

I Asked a Scarecrow in Out of the Snow

I asked a scarecrow in out of the snow.
'Please be a guest in my house.'

The scarecrow said, 'Can I bring a friend?
For in my sleeve lives a mouse.'

Into the house and out of the snow
Came a small mouse and an old scarecrow.

From another sleeve out popped a shrew.
'Excuse me,' it said, 'but can I come too?'

Into the house and out of the snow
Came a shrew, a mouse and an old scarecrow.

Then a tiny voice called from the straw,
'Is there room in your house for just one more?'

Into the house and out of the snow
Came a vole, a shrew, a mouse and scarecrow.

Now the Spider's Web Is Spun

on a currant bun
wise flies
hide in disguise.

Old Lady Ironing

Think'll
iron out
a wrinkle

Playing Football With the Dog

Arthur Sneer played football with his dog.
How nasty can you get?

Dirty Laugh

The reason I've never seen a
Clean hyena
Is because instead of a bath-night
They have a laugh-night.

Sad Kisses

Don't want to kiss anyone ever.
I've seen Mum and Dad do it.
Before you do it
You shout at one another,
Then you hit one another,
Then you cry.
Then you kiss and make up.
Kissing must hurt.
It's horrible.

How the New Teacher Got Her Nickname

When the new teacher said,
'I'm going to be frank with you,'
I burst out laughing.
'What are you laughing about?' she asked.
'It's hard to explain, Frank,' I said.
From that moment on Miss Jones became Frank.
For that, she has me to thank.

'I Want a Word With You Lot ...'

'I want a word with you lot,'
The new teacher said.
Out came the butter,
The knife and the bread,
'We hope the word's tasty,'
The cheeky class said.
'We hope it's not SPROUT,
Or CABBAGE or FISH,
(Or anything healthy poured into a dish).
A good word would be
SAUSAGE, or CHOCOLATE, or PIE,
And CAKE is a word
For which we'd all die.'

'Enough of this nonsense!
I'm fed up, I'm through!
You'll all eat your words
When I'm finished with you.
The word that I want
Is not one word, but two
That when stuck together
Make you feel blue.
You all know it well,
You loathe it, you shirk
From facing up to
That word
                    HOMEWORK.'

Grumbly Moon

'Turn that music down!'
Shouted the grumbly moon to
the rock 'n' roll stars.

Runny Egg

For breakfast I had a runny egg.
I chased it round the table.
It wobbled and it screeched at me,
'Catch me if you're able!'

So I nailed it to the table.

The Cook's Tragedy
A Short Play for Ham Actors

A: I once knew a cook who moved among the cream of society.

B: A good egg?

A: Unfortunately he thought he could have his cake and eat it.

B: You mean he wanted everything on a plate?

A: Exactly. He thought life was going to be as easy as pie.

B: Obviously he never used his loaf.

A: One day, when the chips were down, he turned sour.

B: I suppose he became a fast liver?

A: He didn't give a sausage for anyone.

B: No doubt he ended up in the soup?

A: Of course. He realized his goose was cooked when he heard the police had a bone to pick with him.

B: You mean he was acting fishy and they grilled him?

A: He told them a half-baked story and they gave him a real roasting.

B: Such lives are food for thought.

Hide-away Sam

Hide-away Sam sat in the darkness,
Pale as the day he was born,
A miser who stored up his blessings
Yet looked on blessings with scorn.

He peeked through a chink in the doorway,
A crack on which the sun shone.
All the things he had craved danced past him,
He blinked, and they were gone.

A ladder was stretched up to Heaven,
Its rungs were covered in dew,
At its foot was a bucket of diamonds
(From the sky God had stolen a few)

And beyond the ladder an orchard
Where bees dunked in pollen flew
Between the falling blossom
And the core of a fruit that was new.

'Time to come out and enjoy life!'
A voice boomed down from above.
'Time to swap ten aeons of darkness
For one bright second of love.'

But Hide-away Sam shrank inwards.
He refused to open the door.
The Angel of Mercy lost patience,
Shrugged, and said no more.

Hushabye Lullaby

Listen. Hush.
Don't be hasty.
Something's eating
Something tasty.

In the cupboard
As lights go off
Can't you hear
Moths chomping cloth?

Listen. Hush.
Other sounds
Are moonlight falling
On the ground,

And shadows bumping
Into trees,
And the snoring,
Dreaming bees.

Listen. Hush.
Isn't that
The soft pad
Of the cat?

There are sounds
I am not sure
I have ever
Heard before.

I try so hard
To hear all things
Behind the silence
That sleep brings.

Sleepy-time Crime

I looked in the mirror,
Had a bit of a scare,
For when I looked closer
I wasn't there.

I turned round to find if
I was behind me,
But when I turned round
I couldn't find me.

'I've vanished!' I thought,
'I'm gone for ever!
I shouldn't have been
Such a big bother!

No one will find me
Or miss me or care,
The mirror is empty.
I am not there!'

I pondered and wondered
And then I remembered
The thing I had done
While everyone slumbered:

I'd sneaked from my room
Dressed up as a Viking
To see if my outfit
Was quite to my liking.

I'd adjusted the mirror
On its nail on the wall,
Never expecting
The daft thing to fall.

CRASH! went the mirror,
But nobody had woken.
I picked up the pieces
Of the mirror I'd broken,

Then sneaked back to bed
To worry and sleep,
And then up again
For a guilt-ridden peep.

I wished I had dreamt
That I had broken
The mirror I'd broken
When no one had woken,

But my crime stared me
Right not in the face;
No doubt by tomorrow
I'll be in disgrace.

Rabbit's Spring

Snow
goes,

Ice
thaws,

Warm
paws!

Lunatic

One day I went crazy.
I rushed from room to room shouting, 'Hush!'

Dad was singing in the kitchen.
I made him hush.
The sausages sizzled in the frying-pan.
'Take them off,' I said. 'Hush.'

Mum was hoovering. I flicked off the switch.
'Hush,' I said.

They thought I was mad.
I wasn't. I could hear something.
Something nobody else could hear.

'What is it?' they asked. 'What is it?'

I said, 'Hush.'

So they hushed and we all listened.
They couldn't hear a thing.
'You're barmy,' they said, 'barmy.'

'No,' I said. I was excited.
I could hear my heart.
I could hear a luna
                    tic.

Chaos on the Catwalk

The snake-skin hissed, 'I hate this show!'
The shark-skin said, 'I do too.'
The fox-fur said, 'I concur.
I'm leaving, how about you?'

The clothes the crowd had been wearing
Cried out, 'Enough is enough!
We never wore human flesh –
We can do without the stuff.'

From the seats below the catwalk
There was a sudden uproar,
As with revitalized grins
All the fur-coats and the skins
Rushed out to the exit door.

The audience gaped, astonished,
They didn't know what to do.
'Fashion stinks!' yelled a young lynx,
'Whatever anyone thinks
It's yukky and stinks. Yar Boo!'

The last to leave was a kid-glove,
It cried its way up the aisle
Behind a tatty fur-coat
Made from the skin of a goat
And claws from an old crocodile.

'MY LEATHER TROUSERS ARE GONE!'
'I FEEL CHILLY AND SILLY!'
'I'VE ONLY MY HAT LEFT TO COVER MY
   WILLY!'
'WHERE'S MY LEOPARD-SKIN DRESS!'
'MY BRA'S IN A MESS!'
'PLEASE TURN AWAY, MY KNICKERS LOOK
   GREY!'

You should have heard the commotion.
Everyone felt quite a fool,
Except a young usherette
Who wore a nice cotton dress
And said, 'I couldn't care less.
Killing for fashion is cruel.'

Mooning

What shall we do? O what can we do?
The Man in the Moon has lost his shoe –

We'll search all night on the rubbish-dump
For a star-spangled sneaker or a moon-bright pump.

What shall we do? O what can we do?
Now he's gone and lost his trousers too.

We'll search all night and hope to find
Something that will warm his bare behind.

It's a bit strange and it's a bit sad
But the Man in the Moon has gone quite mad.

He is flinging away all his clothes
And where they'll end up nobody knows,

So don't look at the sky, don't look, it's rude –
The Man in the Moon is completely nude!

Growing Pains

Growing
    bored
Growing
    sad
Growing
    mad
Growing
    batty
Growing
    scatty
Looking
    tatty
Feeling
    ratty
Looking
    frumpy
Growing
    jumpy
Feeling
    grumpy
Growing
    spotty
Growing
    pains

The Church Rat

A rat lived in my brother's shoe,
It was a lonely creature.
I took it to a church one day
And gave it to a preacher.

It ate the bread, it drank the wine,
It nibbled on a cassock,
It grew a little tipsy
And caused a lot of havoc.

'Dear rat, calm down! Control yourself.
You are in the presence of a preacher.'
'I know,' it said. 'In another life
I was the preacher's teacher.'

'I do believe you're right,' I said.
'There's a similarity in the way
You hold your paws and he his hands
When you both bend down to pray.'

The Secret Prayer

There's a prayer I never tell my mum and dad.
Even when I hate them, I say it just the same.
'Dear God,
Don't ever let them die, or if you do
Make sure I go too.
Or better still, wait until I'm gone
Then let them follow on –
Because without them Heaven would
Not be half so good.'

The Wicked Priest

One Sunday morning in between
A sombre prayer and hymn,
A priest went and changed the gospel
Regardless of the sin.

He said there were three brothers
With bags and bags of loot,
And the wisest one among them
Buried it in a boot.

Then late one night that naughty priest
With spade clutched in hand,
Sneaked around the parish gardens
And dug up two hundred grand.

He blessed his sheep and locked the church
And then he sneaked away
To lead the life of happiness
That comes to those who pray.

He might not get into Heaven.
He might end up in Hell,
But meanwhile he's happy living
At Paradise Hotel.

Michael Monday

Born on Monday, Tuesday see
Me going to the nursery.
Wednesday finds me at the gate
Of the school I love to hate.
Thursday finds me blushing pink.
(I'm in love again, I think.)
Fridays finds upon my knee
A child that belongs to me.
By Saturday I'm wrinkling up,
On Sunday I run out of puff.
Then Monday comes around again
And I am free of Sunday's pain.
Now I am another thing
And sit up in a tree and sing,
And see the world a different way
To how I did yesterday.

Blind Hope

A frog crawled out the marshland,
Sat on a mound of earth,
To the creatures around him
He boasted of his worth.

'I'm a fantastic doctor,
There's nothing I can't heal,
If any of you are sick
To me you can appeal.'

The animals stared amazed
At his blotched, spotty skin,
At his huge and bulging eyes
And legs so long and thin.

'Boastful fool, go crawl back home –
You ought to see your face!
You're a small and slimy frog
That ought to know its place!'

His puffed-up pride was injured,
He thought them most ill-bred,
He turned to face them slyly
And this stark truth he said:

'No doubt there will come a day
When no doctor is near –
Then you'll forget I'm a frog –
Blind hope will drive you here.'

Why Toads Look Much More Serious Than Frogs

Frogs on logs
between croaks
crack jokes.

It tantalizes
flies and
loads of toads.

In their abodes
between croaks
these sombre blokes
analyse the jokes.

What Do You Want With Your Chips?

Do you want cat stew with mint sauce,
    putrid plums and cream,
Or custard-coated crushed canaries
    held in high esteem?

We can serve hedgehog and fried figs
    or poodle-pup pie,
Or a rack of roasted rats' tails
    straight from Paraguay.

... er, I think I'll just have the chips, please.

Mrs Siatic and the Bullies

Stiff and rheumatic is old Mrs Siatic,
The poor lady's bent double and grey.
She hates where she lives because of the kids
Who mock her and then stroll away.
If you tied knots in their veins
And poured into their brains
The kind of cruel pain she must live with,
Perhaps then they'd be kinder
And then they might find her
A happier neighbour to live with.

Bits and Pieces

When Uncle Fredrick passed away
It really broke our hearts,
He loved going to the hospital
To be fitted with spare parts.

After the wake we made a list
Then sat about and mused
Over all the bits and pieces
That might still be used.

We set out to find them.
It caused no great alarm
To find in the cupboard
His artificial arm.

'Three cheers for Uncle Fredrick!'
Was the merry mourners' shout.
'We've found a bit of Fredrick.
Now there's less to grieve about.'

We searched inside the cupboard
To dispel our lingering grief,
On the bottom shelf we found
A set of stained false teeth.

This cheered us up no end
And with less reason now to weep,
We tiptoed back into the room
Where Fredrick used to sleep.

On the bedside table
It came as no surprise
To find inside a glass jar
A spare set of his glass eye.

Then from downstairs we heard
Another 'Hip hurray!
It's not the cat Gran's trodden on,
It's Fredrick's old toupee!'

But our excitement was diminished
And our eyes began to smart,
When we found the missing valve
From Uncle Fredrick's heart.

Still, we piled what we had gathered
In the centre of the room.
There were enough bits and pieces
To disperse the gloom.

So hip hip again for Fredrick,
If we go on like this
There will be nothing much of Fredrick
To either mourn or miss.

Spider Apples

Someone told me recently
That I should never go
Into the glittering orchard
Now thick with frozen snow,

For there I'd meet a spider
Who would offer me
Frost-scented, ice-rimmed apples
Plucked from a burning tree,

And if I were to taste one
Then I would never be
Free of that glittering orchard
Where weird apples grow

And a cloven hoof-print
Is marked clearly in the snow.

Aphasia*

I'm seven, and I'm dead bright,
But words give me a fright.
Words are bullies.
Sneaky things. They gabble and lie.
Sometimes trying to understand them
Makes me cry. Words hurt.
Words are all over the place,
They get shoved in my face.
I don't know why but
Words make me cry.

I wish words were things
You could hug,
Or that they smelt nice.
I wish they came in bottles
Like fizzy drinks, or melted
Like ice-cream. But they don't.
Words are mean. They bully me,
Lock me away
From what I want to say.

*Aphasia is a condition that makes it difficult for people to understand
or learn speech. It causes great distress. This poem was written for the
Association of All Speech Impaired Children.

I can't even ask for help
And I'm only seven
(And a bit).
Words spread nasty gossip.
They must. Otherwise why
Would people think I'm thick.

Words,
They make me sick
Inside.

Some Rhymes Are a Sight and Some Are Really Sound

It's a pity the sound of *cough*
Won't rhyme with *rough*.
It's tough.
And it's a bother that *Dover* and *cover*
Don't suit one another
While *clover* and *Rover*
Rhyme over and over.
It's weird
How *weird* and *beard* look different but heard
Fit like hands in a glove
Or like a dove in love with above.
It's odd
How *pot* and *lot* both rhyme with *squat*
But *squat* will not
Rhyme with *cat* despite the *at*.
Fancy that!

And though there's no *y* in *high*
It still rhymes with *fly*
And so will *sky* unless an *i*
Replaces the *y*
Which makes it *ski*
Which rhymes with *me*, you see?
The last example I'll cite
Is how *site* and *sight*
Both rhyme with *might*,
Though on the page *might*
Might look a sight
If rhymed with *cite*
So I'll put out the light.
Good-night!

Winter Variations

GRASSHOPPERS

Grasshoppers bending blades of grass
Tomorrow will be coated in snow,

However much you want them to stay
The wind will snatch their songs away.

LEAVES

I heard the trees whispering, each tongue was a leaf,
And what they were whispering was, 'Stop, thief!'

Behind them Jack Frost was hurrying away.
In his hands each leaf had begun to decay.

BEES

Flightless bees, numbed by cold,
Leave winding trails in the sparkling frost,
Winter's a maze in which they're lost.

GOLDFISH

Beneath a sheet of milky ice,
Transformed by a wintry wand,

I saw phantom goldfish floating
Like sunken treasure in the pond.

My Sister, My Brothers, Christmas and Me

The reason our Cathy's crying
Isn't hard to understand,
She tugged at Santa's beard
And it came off in her hand.

When we dragged her out the grotto
We passed a butcher's shop.
She saw a row of headless turkeys
And then she cried non-stop.

It's Christmas! It's Christmas!
We're going to have some fun,
Mum is in a panic
And it's only just begun.

The goose is in the oven,
And so's the budgie too –
Its cage was opened by mistake
And that is where it flew.

A robin from the garden
Hopped in on to the mat.
It looked just like a Christmas card,
But now it's in the cat.

There'll be a thousand mince-pies
And lots of cream to lick,
There'll be so much of everything
I'm bound to get quite sick.

There'll be tangerines and walnuts,
Brandy pudding too,
Chocolate-coated angels
And toffees to chew.

Best of all would be a snowman
But I don't remember snow,
I've never thrown a snowball –
It's a pleasure I don't know.

It might be the Global Warming.
(It could be pretty grim
If the ice-caps went and melted
Before I learnt to swim.)

Last year I got a boring book
From awful Aunty Jane,
This year I'm going to wrap it up
And send it back again.

For my little sister Cathy
I don't know what to get.
I'd rather just wrap her up
And send her to the vet.

For my horrid little brother
I've made an iron box.
I'm hoping he'll crawl into it
(It's got ten child-proof locks).

I'm fed up with their fingerprints
On the Christmas cake,
And the way they think all my toys
Were bought for them to break.

I wish Santa would come early
And put them in his sack.
He could take them to the North Pole
And never bring them back.

He could leave them in an igloo,
I'm sure no one would care.
They'd make a rather tasty snack
For a hungry polar bear.

My older brother scoffs at me.
He's made a nasty trap.
He says if Santa *does* exist
We're bound to hear it snap.

I've just written off to warn him,
And have explained how to defuse
The electric cable on the roof
My brother says he'll use.

He'd demobilize the reindeers,
Fry Santa in his sleigh,
He'd do some really wicked things
If he could have his way.

But Christmas is a time of love,
And so we've called a truce.
Now everyone will be happy . . .
Except for the goose.

Hippo-rhyme-opotamus

'I'm sick to death,' the hippo said,
'I tell you, there are times
I'd like to crush those awful poets
And all their silly rhymes.
It really is undignified
The way they rhyme my name.
I wish I was magnanimous
But I feel venomous
When my name's made autonomous
With people like Hieronymous.
It's absolutely scurrilous
How their half-baked rhymes mock at us
Harmless hippopotamus.'

Small Wonders

Brand-new elephants roamed through the jungles.
Brand-new whales splashed down through the oceans.
God had slapped them together,
Happy as a kid making mud pies.

He wiped His hands clean.
'Now for the hard part,' He thought.
He took his workbench into the garden.
Delicately He placed in the bee's sting,
The moth's antenna,

His hand
Not trembling in the slightest.

Don't Forget to Wash Behind Your Hearing-aid!

It's hard getting your own back on groan-ups.
I always thought
one of the best things about
being grown up would be
getting my own back on those who
had been nasty to me.
But groan-ups cheat.
While you are busy growing up
they think: 'Hu, hu, there's that boy
I was nasty to, and he's nearly
old enough to get his own back!'
They feel they're under attack
and start to shrink. I think
they do it on purpose. They get
all frail and wizeny-looking
and you just can't go around
getting your own back on little old ladies
and wrinkly little men

who were nasty when
you were ten.
You can't twist their ears
or shake them by the shoulder
and shout, 'Take your teeth out!
Brush them immediately!
You'd better obey me!'
or
'Don't forget to wash behind your hearing-aid!'
The trouble is you don't even want to.
Groan-ups always win.
It's one of the hard, hard facts of life.

The Devil of a Cook

I've never cooked a crocodile,
I'm not partial to boiled bear,
I've never fried a fox-cub
(Think of all that fur).

I've never whisked a weasel
Or mashed a mongoose,
I've never poached a pelican
In the bladder of a moose.

I've never sautéd snakes
Or guzzled grilled gazelle,
I've never tried to toast
A tortoise in its shell.

Liquidizing lizards
And microwaving mice
Might be stylish cooking
But they don't taste very nice.

Grating baby glow-worms
Or mincing death's-head moths
Does nothing for my tastebuds.
(I can't stand insect broths.)

Though I've baked a badger
And casseroled a chimp,
Sitting down and eating them
Would make my bowels go limp.

I'm the devil of a cook,
The animals know me well.
I fry their souls for breakfast
In my kitchen down in hell.

Deep-fried Nightmare

In the local beak-smackin' Deep-fried Human Shop
I asked for something tasty, said, 'How about a chop?'

The chicken that was serving dished up food non-stop,
'Do you want one on its own?' it asked, 'or with peas
  on top?'

'How about the taste?' I asked. 'I'm not exactly sure
I fancy eating humans. I've not tried one before.'

'They taste like your mother, they taste like your dad,
They're as tender as your sister, in fact they're not that
  bad.'

I dithered and dawdled, not sure what to eat.
The animal behind me suggested human feet.

'They have a decent flavour, especially the toes.
They're my favourite bit of humans – I'm having two
  of those.'

In the local beak-smackin' Deep-fried Human Shop
I saw a plate of baby's brains with hot sauce on top.

Of course it was a nightmare, I'd not gone insane,
But still I won't be eating take-aways again.

The Soldier's Shoe
After a poem by Morgenstern

Along the road one cold war-torn dawn
Wandered a shoe with an old shoe-horn.

The shoe was empty but with a cough
It begged and pleaded, 'Please pull me off.'

The shoe-horn said, 'Hang on a minute,
You're just a shoe with nothing in it,

I do not want to be cruel, or scoff,
But there's nothing left to pull you off.

The reason you look bloody and red
Is that your foot's been blown up, it's dead.'

The shoe said, 'Fancy that, well I'm blowed!'
And they continued on up the road.

Little Miss Look-at-me

I went for a picnic,
I went down to the beach,
I was going to have a lazy day
Until I heard that screech:

'Look-at-me!'

It was Little Miss Look-at-me
She was yelling all the time,
'Look-at-me! Look-at-me!'
As if it were a crime
To look at something else instead
Of looking all the time
At that little prima donna
Who thought she was sublime.

She was splashing in the water,
Moving out of reach,
Ignoring all the children
Scrambling for the beach

Because . . .

QUICK! GET OUT THE WATER!
'Look-at-me! Look-at-me!'
WILL YOU SHUT UP AND LISTEN. THERE'S A
'Look-at-me! Look-at-me!'
HUGE SHARK COMING AND IT'S
'Look-at-me! Look-at-me!'
GETTING CLOSER AND
'Look-at-me! Look-at-me!'
CLOSER AND
'Look-at-me! Look-at-me!'
ITS TEETH ARE SHARP AND WHITE AND

                            Whoops!

Little Miss Look-at-me
In the belly of a shark,
Haven't heard a word from her
And it's getting rather dark,

So think I'll go back home
And take a nap in bed,
Now there's no more Miss Look-at-me
Jangling in my head.

You Can't Be That

I told them:
When I grow up
I'm not going to be a scientist
Or someone who reads the news on TV.
No, a million birds will fly through me.
I'M GOING TO BE A TREE!

They said,
You can't be that. No, you can't be that.

I told them:
When I grow up
I'm not going to be an airline pilot,
A dancer, a lawyer or an MC.
No, huge whales will swim in me.
I'M GOING TO BE AN OCEAN!

They said,
You can't be that. No, you can't be that.

I told them:
I'm not going to be a DJ,
A computer programmer, a musician or a beautician.
No, streams will flow through me, I'll be the home of
    eagles;
I'll be full of nooks, crannies, valleys and fountains.
I'M GOING TO BE A RANGE OF MOUNTAINS!

They said,
You can't be that. No, you can't be that.

I asked them:
Just what do you think I am?
Just a child, they said,
*And children always become
At least one of the things
We want them to be.*

They do not understand me.
I'll be a stable if I want, smelling of fresh hay,
I'll be a lost glade in which unicorns still play.
They do not realize I can fulfil
Any ambition.
They do not realize among them
Walks a magician.

The Irreplaceable Mum

If you were a crack in a mirror,
If you were a flea on a cat,
If you were a slug in a jug,
I'd still love you, I wouldn't mind that.

If you were a smudge on a picture
Or an opera singer struck dumb,
If you were a pain in the neck then
You'd still be my very best chum.

If you were a fly in a pizza,
If you were a difficult sum,
Even if you were humpy and grumpy
You'd still be irreplaceable, Mum.

Short-sighted Sergeant Urgent
or, Detergent's No Deterrent

Sergeant Urgent swiftly shopping
Through the supermarket rushing,
Among the soap suds and detergent
Found a packet marked 'deterrent'.

He shouted out to the shoppers,
'This'll put the cop back into coppers!
It'll rub the rob right out of robbers
And a million other thieves and bothers!'

Excitedly, Sergeant Urgent
Bought ten tons of the detergent.
Poor short-sighted Sergeant Urgent,
He used it all but sad to say
The crooks he caught got clean
                    away.

The Utter Butter Nutter

Herbert Niggins was a nutter,
On the staircase he spread butter.
We knew he was a real twit
When he went and slipped on it.

Llama Calmer

Never alarm a harmless llama
But try to calm an alarmed llama
Because a calm llama will never harm a
Hair on the head of a llama calmer.

I asked a groan-up if he knew
Why most groan-ups were boring.
He didn't hear a word I said –
He was too busy snoring.

The Big Question

At the back of my mind a question's gnawing:
Why are most groan-ups so boring?

If you know the answer please
Put your mouth to a groan-up's ear and sneeze.

The Rival Arrives

Tom, take the baby out the fridge
And put the milk back in.
We know you are not used to him
And think he makes a din,
But I'm afraid he's here to stay
And he is rather cute,
So you'll have to stop insisting
He goes in the car-boot.
And please stop telling all your friends
We bought him in a sale,
Or that he's a free sample
We received in the mail.
He was *not* found in a trolley
At the local Mothercare,
And a family did not give him us
Because they'd one to spare.

You should look on the bright side, Tom.
In just a year or two
You will have someone else to blame
For the wicked things you do.

Sally Slipshod

Miss Sally Slipshod lost her memory
One bright sparkling autumn day,
Tried to pick up a burning sunbeam,
Was amazed it got away.

Saw a birch tree; thought it a fountain
Tumbling through the space between
The garden wall and rhododendron
Where the birch tree had once been.

She mistook a child for an angel,
Mistook a rose for its wounds;
The busy world's bald din and clatter
Was transformed to tinkling sounds.

The dawn transformed earth's clods to diamonds,
Wind orchestrated the bars
Of the spiky branches in which clung
The frosty blossoms of stars.

These were the things her memory clung to,
The rest she let fall away.
She saw God's kind face in each spider's;
She knelt among them to pray.

When darkness fell she did not see it;
Saw only light flowing there.
'Your mind has gone wrong,' people warned her.
Sally Slipshod did not care.

How could dull people comprehend her?
Ears so sharp they could unveil
The sound of water in a mountain
And from two miles the nightingale.

Miss Sally Slipshod lost the memory
Of all things dark, drab and dull,
And of the prison others made for
All she considered wonderful.

The Family Exchange

While walking home from school one day
I saw, to my surprise,
A sign saying 'Family Exchange'
Blazing before my eyes.

I rushed straight home for Mum and Dad
And thought, 'What a caper!'
I searched high and low until I found
Stacks of plain brown paper.

Excitedly I wrapped them up
And took them to the shop.
'How about these two here,' I said,
'What'll you give me if I swap?'

'We'll give a ton of gold,' they said,
'Two leopards and a talking cat.
We'll give a bunch of fabulous jewels
For parents such as that.'

'If they're worth so much I'll take them back,
They must be the very best.
I'll bring along my brother instead.
Now he is a little pest.'

For him – a can of worms,' they said,
'Two mouse-skins and a bat.
We'll give you a clout on the ear,' they said,
'If you bring a brat like that.'

The World's Most Disgusting Medicine
or, Never Kick the Doctor in the Shin

Dad's after-shave and rattlesnake's spit,
A monkey's tongue (but only a bit),
Super-glue and Bostik, kangaroo vomit,
Maggoty old mole-fur with dead fleas on it.
Snails crushed in pepper-grinders, fungus from a rat,
A milky-white eye from a dead tabby cat,
Slime from the bottom of an old dustbin,
Two little cockroaches crushed up thin,
Juice from a cabbage boiled for a year,
Squishy smelly wax from an elephant's ear.
These are the ingredients the doctor put in
The medicine he gave me when I kicked him in the
   shin.

Progress

Fairyland's not what it used to be.
I went back to take a look.
The butcher's shop
Sells dragon-meat,
The underbelly of the creature's cheap.
Only poor witches buy it.
In their corrugated huts
They fry it, sighing
For the bad old days.

Sandwiches

It's not the sea muttering
Or the crabs carousing,
Or salty shrimps singing
Or flying fish sighing
For all their friends frying –
                              No!
It's sandwiches dancing
And prancing and cackling!
Sandwiches picnicking,
O it's quite sickening
The spells that they're whispering!
'Eat us!' they're muttering
And all the while buttering
Each other and muttering
Strange spells into sea-shells
And what is much worse is
They're cursing the nurses
Who came to the beaches
With children and teachers
And various creatures
Who ate juicy peaches

But left the sandwiches
Curled up at the edges
Alone on the beaches
In sea-storms and blizzards
Nibbled by wizards
Disguised as sand-lizards.
Listen to them calling!
They sound quite appalling:
'O we'll get our own back
When we get our **T** back
Until then the hitch is
We're harmless sandwiches
Instead of SAND WITCHES!'

I Can't Be a Dunce Because...

I gave myself ten out of ten for geography,
For spelling and sums too,
I gave myself ten out of ten for adding an 0
To everything I do.

Harry the Hatchet

Harry, destructive, extremely invective,
Pimply, bad-tempered and grey,
You're bound to catch it if you use that hatchet
In any unsociable way.

The Daft Owl

Not all owls go
'Tu-whit, tu-whoo'

(It is not something
All owls do).

I knew one whoo
Was tu-whit

less
       tu-
         whoo.

Birds

You might know about the yaffle,
The culver and the widgeon –
All a bit more exciting than
That boring bird, the pigeon.

How about the cassowary?
The apteryx? The moa?

Those flightless birds next to whom
Most others run much slower.

There is nothing beats the eagle,
Or the falcon or the kite,
When it comes to acrobatics
They excel themselves in flight.

Some other birds mistrust the sky
And think that water's grander.
I am thinking now of the swan,
The ouzel and goosander.

It is true the parrot's boastful
And speaks a lot of rot
And insists on being filthy
When his owners wish he'd not.

He's really not my favourite bird.
I suppose that at a push
My favourite bird would be the wren
If it sang more like the thrush.

Let's not say much about the dodo,
The poor thing is obsolete.
One reason is because it was
Baked by pirates as a treat.

Today the saddest birds of all
Must be the hen and turkey.
Their dull lives are brief, their futures
Can look extremely murky.

In recent times the safest bird
Has become the cooing dove,
For who on this earth will admit
To a taste for killing Love?

Chilly Hot

Mum said, 'Careful!
Rice is chilly.'
I said, 'No, it's not.
Don't be silly.'
When my mouth caught fire
Mum laughed a lot –
The rice wasn't chilly
But the chilly was hot.

There's an Old Town

There's an old town where nobody goes,
Where nobody lives, where there's never a noise.
We pass through it in motors, above it in planes,
We clatter right past it in the safety of trains.
There's no milkman, no postman, no policeman either,
No schoolyard, or playground, not even a teacher.
Few people go there and none come away,
There's no one to play with at the end of the day.
In it are angels and demons and stones
That lean close together and whisper of bones.

Lettuce Pray

I'm standing here outside the headmaster's office
and it's all because of
that stupid word lettuce
AND IT'S THE WORST PLACE TO STAND IN THE
     WHOLE WORLD!
And it's hard to be fearless and
tearless when you're feeling
helpless and the whole
world feels airless
and it's all because of
that stupid word lettuce!
I'm sure Jesus liked a joke or two
(specially when He was my age),
don't you? And I'm sure He
wouldn't have been angry with me
or made me stand outside
His office all day
just because I said
lettuce pray.
I think I'll tell the Head
I didn't say
lettuce pray –
I'll say I said
lettuce pray
(after all they may).
If there was any justice in this school
the Head would just
lettuce go home

Magic Breath

In the park one winter I was caught out in a storm,
I blew upon my hands – just to make them warm.

Coming home exhausted from a gruelling day at
   school,
I blew upon my soup – just to make it cool.

I must be a magician! Why was I never told
That with a single breath I can
Blow both hot and cold?

Speared Peer
An Elocution Lesson

Last year
on a pier
near Tangier
for reasons unclear
I fear
an austere racketeer
from Agadir
stabbed a peer
in the rear
with a spear.

My Friend Wazinme

'I don't know how he did it,
But my friend Wazinme
Snapped the two main branches off
Dad's brand-new cherry tree.'

'Are you sure it was not you
Who broke the cherry tree?'
'Of course,' I said, 'it was my friend,
You know, it Wazinme!'

The River's Story

I remember when life was good.
I shilly-shallied across meadows,
Tumbled down mountains,
I laughed and gurgled through woods,
Stretched and yawned in a myriad of floods.
Insects, weightless as sunbeams,
Settled upon my skin to drink.
I wore lily-pads like medals.
Fish, lazy and battle-scarred,
Gossiped beneath them.
The damselflies were my ballerinas,
The pike my ambassadors.
Kingfishers, disguised as rainbows,
Were my secret agents.
It was a sweet time, a gone-time,
A time before factories grew,
Brick by greedy brick,
And left me cowering
In monstrous shadows.
Like drunken giants
They vomited their poisons into me.
Tonight a scattering of vagrant bluebells,
Dwarfed by those same poisons,
Toll my ending.

Children, come and find me if you wish,
I am your inheritance.
Behind the derelict housing-estates
You will discover my remnants.
Clogged with garbage and junk
To an open sewer I've shrunk.
I, who have flowed through history,
Who have seen hamlets become villages,
Villages become towns, towns become cities,
Am reduced to a trickle of filth
Beneath the still, burning stars.

Dad Remembers His Schooldays

When the teacher who used
To yell at us and cane us left
We held a secret collection.
Billy Owen passed around
A brown paper bag.
We filled it, hardly able
To keep straight faces.
At the very last second of
The very last minute of
The very last hour of
The spring term,
We sneaked our bag of gifts
Into his desk and flowed
Out of the school-gates and into summer.
The bag contained a crushed earwig,
A pen-nib, fingernail cuttings,
A rude drawing, a dead wasp,
And, weird as it may sound,
A moth's wing found
In the playground.
Screwed up inside the bag
Was a note saying,
'Good riddance to that pain,
Mr McCane.'

The next term he was gone.
The paper bag was gone.
Life went on.
It was only years later that,
Quite suddenly, I remembered him –
Not as the giant, fearsome McCane,
But as a little man,
Mean and thin.
And I wondered what became of him,
And how he must have felt
When he found our gifts,
The tokens of the esteem
In which we held him.
I felt sorry for him.
You see, by then I had forgotten
The sting of his cane.

Thawing Frozen Frogs

Last autumn Jimmy, for a wheeze,
Tried out our mum's new deep-freeze.
He suddenly made up his mind
To freeze all the frogs he could find.
He packed and stored them all away,
Then brought them out again today.
But he lost interest and grew bored
The very moment that they thawed.
For they did not blink or croak or leap
And from their mouths there seemed to seep
Some disgusting slimy matter
That leaked into Mum's cooking batter.
She found the frogs and, feeling sick,
Rushed to the bathroom rather quick.
You should have heard the way Dad roared,
'Scrape those frogs from the draining-board!'
After Dad's investigation
Other crimes came to attention
And in between protests and wails
Jimmy dug out the worms and snails.

Stuck-up

The fun-fair's real fun, it's real colourful
But I do wish I felt a bit calmer,
For I'm stuck on the Big Wheel
   In

       a

           storm

               and

                   I squeal

                       As

                          I

                             Look

                                 Down

                                     On

                                       The

                                         Whole

                                           Pan

                                              o

                                               ram

                                                 a

The Pint-sized Ark

William stood in the encroaching dark
Banging nails into a pint-sized Ark.
People gathered round him and they mocked
Each single nail mad William knocked
Into the Ark, the pint-sized Ark,
Standing in the encroaching dark
Between the tower-blocks and park.

William, banging, what's it for?
Don't you know it's been done before?

A policeman came, and he made a note:
'It's hardly the size of a rowing-boat.
The Ark's so small he will hardly get
Himself in along with the family pet.'

True, thought William, but my soul will fit,
And that's all I need get into it.

BANG BANG drip BANG BANG drip
BANG drip BANG BANG drip BANG drip

His face was vacant, in his eye was a spark,
And his hammer beat in time to the encroaching dark.

Naughty Nancy Noah

Three by three they came in,
All the clatter, all the din!
Two for the world when it was dry,
One to boil or bake or fry.
Mrs Noah had a cooking-pot
And she served up dinner piping-hot.

Three by three they came in,
Some were fat and some were thin.
The couples were easy but it was harder
Getting the rest into the larder.

'Hurry along! Walk! Don't fly!'
Said this evening's pigeon-pie.
'You hop first.' 'No, after you,'
Said tomorrow's rabbit-stew.

Three by three they came in,
All the clatter, all the din!
Two for the world when it was dry,
One to boil or bake or fry.
Mrs Noah had a cooking-pot
And she served up dinner piping-hot.

Unstable Mabel

Mabel's unstable, be careful, beware
Of that look in her eyes that says, 'I don't care.
I'll do what I want, however unfair.'
Mabel's unstable, and isn't all there.
Mabel's unstable, and able I'm sure
To nail up an angel on to the back door.
Somebody must take her far, far away.
That's what we long for, and pray for each day.
No one remembers from where Mabel came.
Found on the doorstep and brought in from the rain
She sat in a corner, glowered and moaned,
'I was raised by a man whose head was horned.'
Mabel's unstable and if you want proof
Look down at her foot. You'll find only a hoof.
Her eyes are ablaze, like cinders, like fire,
And her dark hair is tangled like razor-sharp wire.

To Join Our Club

To join our club you've got to
Climb a mountain, swim a sea,
Be back home in time for tea.

Easy

That's just the first thing.
To join our club you've got to
Pull a bulldog by the tail,
Catch and eat a garden snail.

OK

That's just the second thing.
To join our club you must
Thrill a gorilla, whack a yak,
Paint your bedroom entirely black.

No problem

That's just the third thing.
To join our club you must
Nail a pixie to a rose,
Twist its ear and pick its nose.

I'll do it right away

That's just the fourth thing.
To join our club you must
a) Be kind to your sister.
b) Wash up after supper.
c) Do your homework.
d) Not watch so much TV.

That's not the club for me.

First Love

Sarah's my girlfriend,
Without her I feel
Like a ball with no bounce,
A shoe with no heel,
An up with no down,
A snow with no flake,
A fish trying to swim
In a waterless lake.
Sarah's my girlfriend,
Without her I fear
I feel that I'm nowhere,
Especially not here.

Dear Mum,

while you were out
a cup went and broke itself,
a crack appeared in the blue vase
your great-great grandad
brought back from China.
Somehow, without me even turning on the tap,
the sink mysteriously overflowed.
A strange jam-stain,
about the size of a boy's hand,
appeared on the kitchen wall.
I don't think we will ever discover
exactly how the cat
managed to turn on the washing-machine
(specially from the inside),
or how the self-raising flour
managed to self raise.
I can tell you I was scared when,
as if by magic,
a series of muddy footprints
appeared on the new white carpet.
I was being good
(honest)
but I think the house is haunted so,
knowing you're going to have a fit,
I've gone over to Gran's for a bit.

Mr and Mrs No

Mr and Mrs No had nowhere to live,
They had nothing to do and nothing to give;
They lived in no house in no pleasant street,
And had nowhere to go and no one to meet.
They did nothing wrong and they did nothing right,
Nobody saw them or knew them by sight,
When dawn came around they were nowhere about;
If they ever existed, nobody found out.

Index of First Lines